OFF BALANCE

DEVIL'S HANDMAIDENS MC ALASKA CHAPTER
BOOK 0.5

E.M. SHUE

Mountain
ROSE
PRESS

Off Balance

Text Copyright ©2023 E.M. Shue

All rights reserved. This book or parts thereof may not be reproduced in any form, stored in any retrieval system, or transmitted in any form by any means—electronic, mechanical, photocopy, recording, or otherwise—without prior written permission of the publisher, except as provided by United States of America copyright law. For permission requests, write to the publisher, at "Attention: Permissions Coordinator," at the address below.

This is a work of fiction. Names, characters, places, and incidents either are the products of the author's imagination or are used fictitiously. Any resemblance to actual persons, living or dead, businesses, companies, events, or locales is entirely coincidental.

Cover Design and Formatting by Mountain Rose Press

Editing by Nadine Winningham of The Editing Maven

Cover and Interior Photos from DepositPhoto

www.authoremshue.com

emshue.ak@gmail.com

OFF BALANCE

Reaper's life is made up of lies, his identity fake. For twelve years, Klay Ulrich has been deep undercover masquerading as the road captain for the Drago Defiance MC. His assignment is to bring down human traffickers running in motorcycle clubs. But when his eyes land on the beautiful wallflower from the Devil's Handmaidens, something in him shifts. For the first time in a long time, he wants someone to know the real him. Reaper's new mission is to make the quiet artist his while carrying on with his directive.

River "Jinx" Schmidt lives her life behind the scenes, quietly creating her art. Racing is the only thing that gets her out of the shadows and gets her blood pumping. When her club asks her to meet with the road captain from Drago Defiance MC to go over the upcoming racing season, she doesn't expect the intense connection. Reaper is big, dominating, and in complete control of every beat of her heart and the breath from her body. Jinx is suddenly finding racing isn't the only thing she craves.

When Reaper and Jinx find themselves stuck in a small town, locked down for twenty-four hours, Reaper will seize his chance and put everything on the line. But when they return to their normal lives, Jinx will have to deceive her club and best friend in order to protect Reaper's secrets and him.

ONE

RIVER

EIGHTIES ROCK MUSIC blares through my headphones as I move down the back roads toward the clubhouse. Tonight the girls and I are going to a bar so I can meet with the Drago Defiance MC Road Captain. They want me to race for them for the upcoming season. There's some guy who wants to sponsor a nitro bike and wants me to ride it. I've seen the DDMC around. Most of the guys are former military. Nothing major came up in their criminal backgrounds when we ran our research. They are all fairly clean.

I come into the turn before the clubhouse and twist the throttle, taking it at a dangerous speed.

Disappointment hits me for a brief moment when I come around the corner. Sometimes I wish I would crash and it all be over with. Every day I question why I'm alive and my parents are not. Why did they have to die so soon?

It's been years since I lost them, and I still feel the pain. No matter how much time has passed or how many MC sisters I now have, I still feel lonely. I've only shared these private thoughts with one person, and she's the reason I'm here. My best friend and her daughter, Skyler, are the reason I wake up every morning and push through the darkness. They are why I live now. When I look into Skyler's eyes, the questions in my mind of my own existence stop. I'm here to help my best friend raise her little girl. A little girl she had when we were both still young ourselves.

I look out over the rolling hills that blend into the Cumberland Mountains. The orange and red colors of fall make the hills look like they are on fire, while the gold of the mountaintops looks like molten liquid. I never thought I'd live in Widow's Creek, Kentucky. It's as far from my small town of Ptarmigan Falls, Alaska, as I could get. When I lost my parents at sixteen, I wasn't sure what I was going to do. All I knew was I couldn't stay there. I had to get away from the memories. The love they had not only for each other but for me was palpable, and I could feel myself drowning in it. I knew Scout couldn't handle the changes in her life without me, so I jumped on a plane and was southbound before I could question my decision. Her uncle had helped me get emancipated, and another family member of hers took me in while I got on my feet. I finished high school and college before I got a job helping Scout in her shop. Now I'm one of the most sought-after automotive painters.

As I approach the turnoff for the clubhouse, I slow down and take the gravel road fast enough that my back tire slips slightly to the side. I learned to ride motorcycles when I was a kid. My father used to race bikes at Tanacross, and now I do the same here for other clubs. Being on a bike is second nature to me. I trust it more than being in a cage. I don't even own one. I borrow Scout's or Violet's if I need one for something. I could've had my father's classic car, but I sold it after he died. I couldn't look at the 1969 Chevy Chevelle SS without remembering all of the times he and I had worked on it together. It was the first car I ever painted. He let me do the rally stripes on it. He had even let Scout work on it once in a while. Other than my mom and me, his Chevelle was his pride and joy. Someday I'll regret selling it, but it was too much then.

All the bikes are parked in front of the clubhouse. Scout's Indian is sitting in the lineup. I don't go anywhere without Riddler—Scout's road name—if I don't have to. I'm pretty much a homebody or a recluse. I can usually be found in my studio, the paint booth at the shop, or spending time with Scout and Skyler. I hate crowds, but I'm here because Brazen, our club president, called and said all hands on deck. Drago Defiance is new to racing, and to be honest, they have a sweet machine I can't wait to get between my legs.

Scout and I have been best friends since elementary school when my parents relocated to Ptarmigan Falls. My father was stationed at the Army base in Fairbanks, and my parents decided to settle down and raise me in one place. Even back then, Scout was a grease monkey. Now she and I run one of the most popular cycle and automotive restoration garages in the area. She knows motors inside and out. She knows them better than people sometimes. I've been an artist since before I could walk, according to my mom. I paint and design. I see what I want the tank or body to look like and then I just do it. It's natural for me to have a paint brush or airbrush gun in my hand. There's callousing on my fingers from my hard work, and I don't care.

I'm not the pretty, sweet girl most guys like, but I don't lack for male companionship either. I'm taller than average at five foot nine. My mother was from Puerto Rico, and my father was Texan with some American Indian in him. I inherited his height and stronger features, and my mother's long, thick black hair and curves. I don't go out looking for men a lot, mostly because I have different needs. I'm scared to tell a man what I really want and like, so I just suffer through sex. Some idiots think Scout and I are a couple because neither of us seek out sex. She struggles with trust issues due to her exes. Skylar's father betrayed her, and the next guy she dated beat her so badly he nearly killed her.

I pull off my helmet when I hop off my bike, leaving the bandana over the top of my head so my curly hair doesn't go crazy everywhere. Riddler walks out with Ginger close on her heels. Ginger is taller than me and working her way into being an enforcer. Her long red hair is pulled back into a ponytail at the base of her skull with a leather wrap around it. I changed at the shop, and we all three look pretty similar dressed in all leather. Scout is very petite compared to Ginger and me.

"Ready, Jinx?" Riddler calls me by my road name and moves to her bike.

"You got this, girl." Ginger thumps me on the back, and I shake my head.

"Riddler, Jinx, and I will go in first. The rest of you give us about fifteen," Brazen orders.

I flip my long leather clad leg over my bike and slip on my helmet again. I know Ginger doesn't like this plan. She likes to forget that Riddler and I are trained as much as she is in martial arts. I've studied Tae Kwon Do since I was a small kid. Riddler learned Krav Maga after her ex, Phantom, attacked her. I started working out harder with her after that too. I wasn't going to let her be a victim again if I could help it.

We head out to a bar in neutral territory. Bikes are parked all over the parking lot. Not only do we, the Devil's Handmaidens, come here but so do other clubs. All are welcome as long as they don't fight. If you break that rule, you're banned along with your club.

This time when I get off my bike, I pull off the bandana and fluff my curly hair, bringing the curls on top back to life. I bend over and shake out my hair before I rise up and adjust my breasts in my skimpy leather top. I know how to use my assets when necessary.

Brazen leads the way with Riddler and me at her back.

REAPER

EVERYTHING COMES TO A STANDSTILL. I know it sounds strange. I know I sound crazy, but something in the room changes, and I can't put my finger on what it is. The bar is slamming, bikers are mixing with sweetbutts, and townies are wishing they were cool enough to hang with us. It's like any other night, but something in the air has changed. I look across the room and spot the source of the disturbance. A curvy brunette standing with a couple other DHMC riders.

She's dressed in tight as fuck black leather pants that hug her hips and long legs—legs that will look amazing wrapped around my head or hips. My eyes trail up her body from her heavy heeled boots to her leather jacket with a cut over the top. Her jacket is open, exposing her tan abdomen and breast-hugging half shirt. Her breasts are a tad fuller than a handful, and I try not to shift as I think about fucking them. My gaze moves to her full lips. The image of that mouth wrapped around my cock makes me so hard that I'm lost for a moment. Finally I reach her light eyes and find her staring right back at me. She has an eyebrow and nose piercing that both twinkle in the light. I want to know where else she's pierced. She has tattoos similar to mine along the back of her hands and fingers. The black ink against her creamy tan skin calls to me. I want to know why she tattoos such a sensitive area that has to be retouched a lot.

I can't help the crook of my eyebrow as I watch a flush move up her body. It has me wanting to move heaven and earth for this woman. She moves behind Brazen and another rider. This one is a petite blond, but I'm still focused on my raven-haired beauty. Her curly hair bounces as she moves toward us.

I hear Snake's intake of breath, and I turn away from her for a moment. I look at him and find he's staring at her too, but there's something else in his eyes. Something that causes my skin to crawl slightly. Something sinister. He desires her but not like I do. I move my hands to my sides and clench my fists. The women continue across the room toward us, and I know in this moment I'll fuck up the world for her. I'll kill. I'll destroy and blow everything I've done over the last few years for her.

People move out of their way. These women are all trained and skilled in ways to hurt, maim, and kill. I know this. It's why they want me to find out what their agenda truly is. When they come to a stop in front of our table, I stand up and tower over her. I don't take my eyes off her as Brazen talks to Snake and the others. Snake approached our club and asked if he could sponsor our bike, but he wanted to meet the woman our Prez wants for the rider.

She won't look at me now. She keeps her eyes down. A true submission that I doubt others know. She only raises her eyes when a bottle smashes near us. I see her body respond by a slight movement. Her fingers flexing and twitching slightly. I know she's carrying. Just like the petite blonde with her flanking Brazen. Both women aren't nervous but taking in everything. I bet, just like me, they clocked all the exits and entrances as soon as they walked in. They have a list in their minds already of the people to watch out for. She might have been watching me just as I was her, but she was also setting herself up for an escape if necessary.

"This is our rider, Jinx." Brazen's voice breaks through my brain, and I watch as my girl nods slightly.

Snake doesn't miss a thing. "Jinx, lovely to meet you." He tries his southern charm on her, and I want to break the hand he has outstretched for her to shake.

"Yeah," she says softly in a voice that isn't accented. She's a Northerner. She looks down at his hand before looking back up at his face, leaving him hanging. He drops his hand, and I watch as his body tightens in anger.

"This is Reaper. He's with Drago Defiance. It's his crew that currently has the bike I'd like to sponsor. I understand you're a rider. How long?"

Her lips pinch and she looks to Brazen, who nods slightly. I watch her soft-gray eyes cloud over and darken. Her thick sooty lashes close for a moment as she controls her emotions. The blonde touches her arm, and then she turns those now cold stormy eyes on him.

"I've been riding longer than was legal. I've raced nitrous bikes along with fuel and others. You asked for me, so I don't need to prove anything."

"*We* asked for you," I say, my voice gruffer than I intended and full of my need for her. She turns to look at me. "My Prez has seen you race and says you're the one he wants."

"Thank you." Her voice softens. There's only a touch of grit to it now.

I can't stop myself from moving closer to her, and she doesn't step back. I get a whiff of wild roses and it causes my cock to press harder against my zipper.

"How about you and I get a drink and discuss the bike while Brazen and Snake hash out the particulars?"

"No, thank you," she says, and I watch as her eyes drop slowly. She's submitting to me without even trying. I want to touch her skin to see if it's as satiny smooth as it looks.

"No," Snake interjects, and we all turn to look at him. "Instead, Jinx will come to my plantation and finalize the deal."

"No," several people say, including me.

"Then the deal is off." Snake smiles. His grin pinches in a sinister way.

"Give us a moment," Brazen says, then steps away with both women. More Maidens walk in and stand at the entrance. They are preparing for a fight. The need to protect this woman is causing my gut to clench.

When the trio rejoins us, Brazen says they will comply, and I know what I need to do.

"I'll be there too."

"You don't need to be." Snake turns to me, and I see the calculation in his eyes. He thinks if he gets her alone, he can have her. I won't allow that.

"No. It's our bike. She's our rider now. I go." This will be perfect. I need to get this invite for the next step, but I can also protect her.

"Fine. Tuesday. Let's say eleven in the morning, that way it won't interfere with your Halloween plans." Snake gives in, but a look in his eye has me wondering what's going on.

The Maidens all head out after it's determined that Jinx and I will head to his plantation in Pandora. I have a couple of days until I see her again. I want to know more about her, but she leaves without looking at me.

TWO

REAPER

I MOVE my bike through the freeway traffic heading into Louisville. I've kept an eye out for any signs of a tail since I left Widow's Creek. As the next exit approaches, I thread the needle between the cars as I move across several lanes to jump off. I drop my heavy boot to the ground at the stoplight and look around me. I hate coming into town, but my handler insisted on a meet and greet before I go to Pandora. Sometimes they do these random checks to make sure an agent hasn't turned. We've had team members in the past who got into drugs or blew the case or their cover. I need to be very careful during the meeting because I wasn't supposed to go to the plantation, but I wasn't going to let Jinx go by herself.

I've been under for so long, I don't remember a life before this one. As soon as the light turns green, I move toward the industrial district, where I have a warehouse apartment. I'll change out my bike for a different vehicle before heading to the meet. I still don't see anyone behind me, but I circle the area several times before I hit the remote to open the large door. Even the bureau doesn't know I have this location set up. I don't have a family to protect, but I do like my privacy.

As soon as the heavy door closes, I'm off my bike and pulling off my helmet and glasses. I don't have much time to get ready. I spent last night watching over Jinx. I found out more about her and where she works. Things I could do without raising any alarms. I have alerts set to notify me when she leaves her shop and when she gets home. Setting up the cameras late at night and making sure the Maidens' hacker didn't know I was piggybacking off their system wasn't easy, but I did it. Everything important in life shouldn't be easy. My life is proof of that.

I move through my studio apartment and take a quick shower. I brush my hair back and look at myself in the mirror after dressing in a pair of slacks and a button-down shirt.

My hair could use a trim on top. It's getting longer than I like. Between it and all my tattoos, I still look like what I am. A road captain for the Drago Defiance Motorcycle Club. I wonder what Jinx thought of me. I don't look like the young naïve agent who started with the ATF all those years ago. When I left foster care, I knew I wanted to do something that would prevent other kids from growing up like I did. I joined the military but was recruited by the ATF a couple of years later. They liked that I had no one. I liked that I could do what I wanted for the most part. Tattoos, piercings, and riding motorcycles, all things I like and enjoy. I've been a real member of the Drago Defiance MC since I prospected at eighteen while in the military. But my brothers don't know what I really am. My Prez knows, and we have an agreement. Nothing concerning the club is revealed unless I have his permission. I've never brought any of the Dragos to justice because they aren't bad, but I hate lying to them. It's a burden I carry with me every day; they are my family.

I keep that secret close to the vest because I do have friends now and don't want to see them get hurt by my decisions. I've been trying to take down a gun runner for the past few years who works with the MCs. Every time I get close, however, something happens. He's crafty and I wonder if he's got someone in the bureau or in the government who is tipping him off. I know working with Snake will lead me to him.

I grab my blazer off the back of the chair and slip it on. As big as I am, I had to have it tailored to size. It's been almost a year since I last wore it. I've been working out more over the last few months and it shows in the stressed seams. I lift the keys for my flat-black F150 FX4 off the board and drop my cell on the counter before I make my way back to the garage. I turned off my phone before I left Widow's Creek just in case someone was tracking me. My secondary phone is in the center console, which I'll turn on once I'm out of the area. During this meeting, I won't be able to keep an eye on Jinx, but I know she'll be safe with her club for a few hours.

After making my way across town, I pull up to the federal building and flash my badge and ID to access the parking garage. Coming in right now is dangerous. If I wasn't as careful as I am, anyone could see me entering the premises, but I've covered my ass as best as I could. With one last glance around me, I exit my truck and make my way inside.

The elevator opens, and I move toward the conference room. People I don't know turn to look at me as I pass. I've been undercover for so long, and I usually meet my handler at a neutral location, so all the staring faces are strangers to me.

"Klay, welcome." My handler smiles at me as I enter the room without knocking. He stands from the other side of the long table. There's a man sitting next to him that I don't know. I don't like surprises.

"Anderson?"

"Oh, let me introduce you to our new division chief, Marik Drawer."

The other man stands and holds out his hand. I shake it and watch as he takes in all of my tattoos. The ink on my head and face, along my neck, my hands, and fingers are all visible. I kept all my jewelry on too. Rings, earrings, nose ring, and leather braided bracelet. I'm not going to change who I really am for anyone.

This is me.

"You might think they aren't professional, but to me they are that along with my own self-expression." I chuckle, trying to make a joke about it.

The new chief isn't amused as he continues to look down his nose at me, which is kind of funny considering he's shorter than me. I size him up like he's doing to me. When he squeezes my hand in an act of intimidation, I can't help the tip of my lip as I give him a little squeeze myself. He pulls his hand back, his eyes flaring. Yeah, don't fuck with me, little prick.

"Please have a seat, *Special* Agent Ulrich." He points to the chair across the table from him and Anderson. He practically spit my title like I don't deserve it.

What the fuck is his problem? I raise my tattooed brow at Anderson in question. My lips are pinched as I take a seat. I wish I had worn all my motorcycle gear for this meeting.

"What's going on, Anderson?" It's best for my anger if I don't acknowledge the asshole.

"Chief Drawer wanted a direct update from you, and I have some of the information you wanted." Anderson points at the file in front of him.

"Before we get to that, Special Agent Ulrich, I'd like to know how much more money we are going to have to sink into this investigation. It's been going on for years. We haven't brought down the Dragons yet, and only a couple of other organizations have seen the inside of prison walls. What about these Handmaidens I've heard so much about? I want an update on your case and what direction you are headed in next." I look over at Anderson, knowing he must be monitoring me more closely than I thought if they know about the Handmaidens.

I lean up in my chair and fold my hands, lacing

my fingers on the table in front of me. LIVE FREE is tattooed across my knuckles, and Drawer looks at them and scoffs. I grind my back teeth in an attempt to control my anger. Jinx's mandala-inspired finger tattoos flash in my mind, and my back straightens. This man is judging me and thinks I'm lacking. The thought of him doing that to Jinx causes instant anger to fill me. She's my girl, and I won't have anyone look down on her.

"Well, Mr. Drawer." I don't address him by his title because his questions confirmed my thoughts. He's nothing but a penny-pinching bureaucrat from DC. He's not an agent and probably never has been.

"That's Division Chief Drawer to you," he spits, and I lean back from the spittle on the conference table.

"Division Chief Drawer, I've helped with the cleaning up of the Hell's Defiance MC. I'm currently working on a gun supplier, who once off the streets will help with shutting down several one percenters. As for the Drago Defiance, they are clean, and I can't infiltrate the Devil's Hand-maidens because they are a women-only club. No men."

"The Dragons, from your previous reports, have drugs and guns. They need to be brought down."

"I won't do that. That's not the deal. I'll bring

down those that deal and sell, but I won't destroy an organization that on the whole is clean. Hell's Defiance only had a few bad apples. When Phantom was sent to prison, it stopped the human trafficking part of their club, and those members we could bring charges against were punished. Those we couldn't, I'm still working on."

"What about these women? Can't you become close to them and put a stop to their clandestine operations?"

I purse my lips as I rub my beard. Not many know about the Maidens' primary function of stopping human trafficking. They are doing good, but they will do it by any means. Playing dumb is going to be my best bet in this situation.

"I don't know what clandestine operations you're talking about." I've never included what they do in my reports. It's not that I'm protecting them. It's that I don't see a need to go against them. They are doing something that the legal system has failed to help with, and that's protecting women all across the United States.

"Everyone knows they have attacked men and are hacking into civilians' emails." He rises from his chair. His anger is a little over the top and makes me question his motives.

"Two of their members testified against Smith and sent him to prison for attempted murder.

That's the only thing I know about them." I wonder for a moment if Jinx knows these members. Names were never released for their protection.

"Yes, but it's the others I want to know more about."

I decide to give him some information, but I don't want to give too much because I don't trust this asshole. "I met with a couple of their members last night. One will be racing our bike in the rallies. Their president was there too. They didn't break the law. If anything, they tried to keep their member away from my target."

"Find out the information and infiltrate them next. I want regular reports on a weekly basis from now on." He leaves the room without saying anything else. Once he's gone and the door is closed, I turn to Anderson.

"What the hell was that?"

"He's been jonesing for these Handmaidens. I don't get it either. I haven't seen anything in your reports that gives us a reason to watch them. They are clean like you said."

"They are." I'm going to have to keep a close eye on this asshole, as well as Jinx. I won't be giving him a complete report next week after our meeting with Snake in Pandora.

Anderson and I talk for a bit more before I head out. He gives me a file on Snake and the crew he's been running with. He doesn't know anything about this plantation in Pandora but said he'd look it up and get back to me this weekend. Monday or Tuesday at the latest.

By the time I return to my warehouse and start the trek back to Widow's Creek, I'm exhausted and don't drive by to check on my girl. I make it home in time to feed my dog, Trigger.

RIVER

IT'S BEEN a couple of days since I saw Reaper, and he's still on my mind. I don't know why I reacted to him the way I did. I wanted to please him. I wanted to submit to him in a way that I've only ever dreamed of. His soulful brown eyes watched me, and I didn't want it to stop. I should've taken him up on his offer for a drink, but I knew Scout would figure out that I liked him if I did that.

Bon Jovi blares through the speakers as I finish working on the swirls of color to make out the Milky Way on the hood of the car. But I'm not seeing that. I'm seeing the black ink of Reaper's tattoos. I'm hearing his voice as he commands me to my knees. I'm feeling his hands squeezing me the way I've wanted for so long.

"River," Mercy hollers my name through the intercom, cutting off the music. "You have a visitor."

I turn to look at the window in the door where they can talk to me via the intercom beside it. There standing looking back at me is Reaper. I lower my air brush gun and remove my facemask along with the hood covering my head. I move to the door and open it up.

"What are you doing here?" I feel my eyes dropping and can't stop the motion. Something about him affects me.

His tattooed fingers slide under my chin and lift it up to look at him. "You missed the message. Snake wants us to come out tonight for a party before the meeting on Tuesday. Said we can stay at the plantation if we want."

I look into his deep brown eyes, and I'm lost for a moment. There's a buzzing in my ears and my legs wobble slightly.

"Jinx, your phone has been blowing up." Another one of the workers pulls me from the fog, and I turn to look at them as I step back from Reaper.

My phone doesn't go in the booth with me. I

leave it on the counter outside the door. I move to it and see the messages from Brazen, Snake, and even Reaper. Snake demanded a contact for me, and I know Reaper took it down too.

"Well, shit." I unzip my suit and pull it off my upper body. I didn't have to come in today because it's Sunday, but I wanted to get my mind off Reaper, and this was the only way. I tie the sleeves around my waist and look out through the bay door as my name is screamed.

"Auntie River." Skyler comes barreling toward me. She's dressed in a cute little miniskirt outfit with a mini leather vest on that claims she's protected by the Devil's Handmaidens. I lift her up into my arms and snuggle her in close. She's a miniature of her mother except for her blue eyes.

"How's my Little Bear doing?"

She wraps her legs around my waist and cocks her head to the side, her long blond hair falling over her shoulder.

"Who's that?" She points to where Reaper is standing behind me.

"I'm Klay, but you can call me Reaper." He holds out his large hand for her to shake. "I'm here to take your auntie on a ride with me."

"Did you ask my mommy's permission?" She pinches her lips and stares him down.

"Little Bear," Scout hollers for her. "Don't bug

your auntie." Scout comes around the corner and sees us standing there.

"I wasn't. He wants to take auntie for a ride."

"Reaper," Scout says as she goes to take Skyler from my arms, but she holds on tighter.

"Auntie, will you tell Mommy I'm old enough to ride my bike in a race like you do."

I look over at Scout, who shakes her head, and I try to hold in my laugh.

"Little Bear, I'll make a deal with you." I twist to set her on the counter as I drop my suit and stand there in my shorts and tank top. I hear what sounds like a growl from behind me and turn to see Reaper checking out my ass. Scout tries to hide her smile behind her hand and moves to the counter, where she hoists herself up to sit next to her daughter. "When I get back from this run, if you can ride the track completely in one go, I'll fight for you." The rally track that we've been taking Skyler to since she was little is a complete motocross track with turns, jumps, and more. She can do each but hasn't tried to do all of them. Both Scout and I make sure she's fully geared up and safe. But she needs to prove she can do it and wants to do it before I give her the reins to race.

"You race motocross?" Reaper moves closer, his hand going to my midback just above my ass.

"Yes. My mommy and aunties have taught me.

Auntie River is the best racer." Her voice is full of pride, and I can't help my shoulders going back and my neck elongating. It fills me with warmth that she's so proud of me.

"I know she is. I've watched her."

My head whips around to look at him, and he smirks as he shrugs.

"Let me run home, shower and pack, then I'll be ready."

I want to say no to Snake, but this is about more than racing. This is about getting into Snake's good graces. Keys, one of our hackers, has found some disturbing online activity that shows he's not only into racing bikes but other illegal activities, including peddling flesh. He traps young girls after getting them addicted to drugs and then turns them out on the street. Sometimes they are underage and runaways. Brazen asked me to go in and find out if he has any at his plantation.

"I'll meet you there," Reaper says, and walks out before I can give him our address.

THREE

REAPER

I KNOW I screwed up when I pulled up to her house and she was watching me. She's dressed in jeans, leather riding chaps, an '80s rock band T-shirt, and a leather jacket with her cut over the top. Her helmet is in her hand, and I see a Harley Davidson Sportster off to the side with a backpack loaded on it. The leather saddle bags appear to be stuffed full too. She moves down the sidewalk to where I'm stopped and braces her legs apart.

"I don't know how you knew where I lived, but you'll forget this place. I don't like others coming here unless I know them."

I slip off my bike and advance on her. I know

what she's doing, and part of me wants to let her push me away because I can't get involved with her. With the division chief on me so hard right now, I probably shouldn't want to get involved with her, but I can't help myself.

We are toe to toe, and I wrap a hand around the back of her neck and tilt her chin up to me. She doesn't move backward or try to fight me. I gently press my thumb and middle finger against her neck tighter at her carotid artery. Her pupils dilate and her body softens. My grip isn't hurting her and won't cause her to go unconscious, but it lets her know I'm with her.

I lean down so my lips move against her ear as I talk to her. "I like to know everything about the people I'm working with. I'm not going to hurt you or your family." I tilt my head toward the house. I know this isn't hers or Scout's place. The house belongs to a Rose Simmons, Scout's aunt and a Devil's Handmaiden. "Your family is safe." I kiss below her ear before I let her go and step back.

Her eyes open and she shakes her body. She turns and walks away from me, and again I know she's putting a wall between us. I'm okay with it this time.

We mount up and head out. The drive to Pandora is only a couple of hours, so we are taking our time and sightseeing. The hills are rolling more as we get closer to our destination and the towns become smaller. Just outside of Pandora, I pull over into a gravel padded area and wait for her to catch up. She fell back a bit ago. It's another way to put a wedge between us. I need her to do it because I'm not strong enough to turn her down. I want her. When I had my hand around her throat, I knew she was it for me. I knew she was perfect for me. A sub that likes breath play. I wonder how much she's explored. The thought of another man dominating her causes my blood to run cold.

I stand from my bike and move to stretch out my long legs. My boot kicks something in the gravel, and I look down to see something sparkling up at me. Squatting down, I brush my gloved hands through the loose rocks and reveal the back of a piece of jewelry. I flip it over and find a four-leaf clover made from green gems. The piece is old and worn. The metal looks like its gold plated, and the green gems look fake in their gaudiness and large size. The diamonds surrounding it are probably cubic zircons or glass.

I hear her bike pull in and shut off. I stand holding the jewelry.

"What's that?" She points to my hand. I look down and shrug before I look back up at her.

"Nothing but some costume jewelry I found lying in the dirt. Bet some old lady is missing her hat pin."

She moves to stand next to me and takes the piece of glass from my hand. She rolls it around in her palm. "This isn't a hat pin. It's a brooch."

Just having her this close to me is causing my body to react. I need to get away from her. I pull the jewelry from her hand and toss it over my shoulder. I don't mean to be rude, but I need the boundaries to be set again. I keep blurring them.

"It's junk. Come on, let's go." I move back to my bike and take off.

I hated doing it, but the more I'm with her, the more I'm willing to say screw it to everything and take her. I don't realize she's not with me for a few moments.

RIVER

I LOOK to where he threw the brooch and then to where he took off. I don't want to be around him anymore than he wants to be around me. I don't know how he knew my secret, but he did. When he grabbed my neck, I was instantly needy for him. My panties almost melted as he whispered in my ear.

I look back to the brooch. Something in me says to go get it. I move off and lean down to pick it up. A tingle works up my arm, and I look around, trying to figure out what the heck is going on. I slip the brooch into my outer pocket and head off to follow him.

When I come up on the Pandora city limit sign, I find Reaper squatting down beside his bike. Just like when I pulled up earlier, his ass in his jeans begs me to run my hands across it. An image of my nails digging into the meaty slabs as he works in and out of my body has my breath catching. I pull over and take off my helmet. For this ride, I didn't wear a full-face helmet. I have my open face style with goggles. The helmet is painted with sugar skulls similar to a couple of my tattoos.

"What's up?"

"It just stalled and won't turn over."

"You put fuel in it?" I ask the obvious question.

He turns on me, that tattooed brow arching behind his aviator sunglasses. "Really?"

"Okay, let me look." I squat down next to him. Looking over the bike, I don't see anything obvious and stand. "Let me try." I throw my leg over his bike and try not to imagine him sitting on this very seat. I turn the key and flip the on switch. I then look at the display that says it's already in neutral. I push the starter. The bike sputters for a split second then dies. I look up at him, and he's smirking at me with a "like duh" expression. "I just wanted to check."

"What? You think I'm lying?" His large arms cross over his chest, and I take in his body. He's in loose low hanging jeans, a T-shirt with a flannel over the top, and his Drago Defiance cut. There's a long Bowie knife on his hip, hanging down his leg. Along his other hip is the chain that attaches to his wallet. His feet shift for a moment, and I realize I'm staring. I swing off the other side of his bike and move away from him. I can't let him affect me. I'm already in over my head with him, and I need to get the information about Snake for the club.

"I'll ride into town and get someone to come help you." I hear the quiver in my voice.

"Don't forget I'm here," he grumbles as he leans against his bike, and I take off. I need to get my feelings for him under control.

I pull over at the first shop I see and have them go rescue him. I don't wait around. I head to the local diner to grab a bite to eat and shake off the urges I have for him. When I pull up, I park my bike out front and switch my helmet for the slouchy beanie I use to cover my hair. It's frizzy from not properly preparing for a ride today.

I sit down in a booth where I can see the shop and watch as the truck pulls up with Reaper's bike in the back of it. When my phone goes off with a message from him, I ignore it and continue to wait for my burger and fries.

I send a quick text to Scout so she knows we made it to Pandora. She and Brazen didn't like the change of plans. But if I pulled out at this point, it would draw more attention to me. I look across the street toward Reaper again. Klay, he said is his real name. I've been on several assignments with the Devil's Handmaidens helping rescue women and children, but this is the first time I've gone undercover like this. I don't want to disappoint anyone.

Sliding my hand into my pocket as I watch Reaper talk to the guy and look at his phone, my fingers touch the brooch. It's warm from being in my pocket. I slip it out and roll it around in my hand. Using a napkin dipped in my water glass, I clean it off. The green gem starts to sparkle. I don't think it's a costume piece. It looks real.

The waitress sets my plate down.

"Where did you get that?" She points at the brooch.

"I found it," I say and hold it out to her. "Do

you know who it belongs to? I want to return it to them."

She backs away from the table. "Food's on us." She points to the brooch. "Take it to the historical society over there. They can help you." She then points across the town square to a large building with stone pillars out front.

I eat my lunch and then drop a twenty on the table before I head out to where she said. If the brooch belongs to someone, I want to return it. I don't want to keep it. I don't need it, and it's definitely not my style.

I look over to see Reaper is still at the shop. He watches me as I walk across the grass of the square. He's talking to another man now instead of the mechanic. My cell goes off again, and I look down.

REAPER
Where are you going?

ME
Going to check out something.

Climbing the steps to the building, I see the words Pandora Historical Society in bold print on the doors. I'm surprised they are open on a Sunday.

The interior is dark, and the place has that old book smell. It's actually calming to my senses. I've always loved to read, and a good old book is the best. Moving to the counter, I reach into my pocket to pull out the brooch. The older woman at the counter takes me in and judges me, as most people do. Not only am I pierced, but I have visible tattoos. Even along my neck. I hold in the disdain I feel when people think they know who I am. I open my fist with the brooch in my palm.

"Where did you get that?" she hisses as she backs up. Her behavior is similar to the server's at the diner. She isn't accusing me of stealing it; it's more like she's afraid of the brooch.

I look down at it and then back at her. "We found it when we were heading into town. My friend found it. He thinks it's a fake."

"Oh, it's not a fake at all." She looks down at the brooch and softly speaks as if she thinks I can't hear her. "I haven't seen it since I was a little girl." She's at least seventy, so that's a long time.

"Then here, you can have it back. I don't want it." I try to hand it to her, but she steps back further.

"No. I can't take it," she practically screams as she holds up her hands in defense.

"I'm not going to hurt you." I lean forward, assuming she's upset with how I look and not the brooch. Who could be afraid of a piece of jewelry? "I didn't steal it. I swear we just found it."

"It's not you. It's that thing." She spits out the last part. "It's cursed. I don't want it. You own it now. Take it with you when you leave. The society has been trying to get rid of it for years."

"But is it historical? What is wrong with it?"

She points to a shelf behind me. "Take one of those green books," she says, and I move to the shelf holding green leather-bound journals. "I won't sell it to you because of that." She indicates the brooch. "If you take that cursed thing out of here, you can keep the book," she says and makes sure she keeps her distance.

I give her my name and information as I take the journal. I flip through a few pages and see the book is copied from an original journal. The title is Brennan Family History, and it has a picture of the brooch on the cover. I turn to see the original journal is on display behind glass on a pedestal. I nod at her and start to move toward the door. I slip both the brooch and the journal into my backpack and stop when Reaper walks in.

"What you got there?" he asks, and I decide not to tell him what's going on.

"Nothing. What's going on with your bike?"

"There are electrical problems. The voltage regulator went out and the stator. They have to have the stator ordered and brought in. It won't be here until Wednesday. Something about the town closing down on Tuesday." His voice must carry because the woman behind the counter responds.

"Yes, Pandora shuts down for Halloween," she says.

We both turn to look at her. "You close down the whole town to celebrate a Hallmark holiday," Reaper growls.

"It's not a Hallmark holiday. It's the rules. Been this way since before I was born. Because we are tired of luck playing in our fates." She points at my backpack where I stored the brooch. "Because of things like that. We don't like the bad luck that will bring. Take it out of here before your luck rubs off on us." She moves away, and I turn to look up at him.

"What are we going to do? We need to get to the plantation, and I don't have a bitch seat on my bike. Plus, I can't stay here indefinitely."

"We have our meeting Tuesday. I've already called Snake. He said to head out."

"You are not riding on my bike," I clarify, and storm out of the building. I don't want him pressed up against my body. The thought of that alone makes my knees weak.

"Are you just going to fucking leave me here?" he says from behind me when I reach the diner, and I turn to look at him.

"Yes." I slip on my helmet and throw my leg over my bike.

"Well, it's a good thing I already lined up a

ride." He moves off toward the man he was talking to earlier and his truck. I can't stop myself from watching as he hops up into the passenger seat. I take off, ignoring my traitorous body. He could have started with that instead of letting me get all worked up and angry.

I head toward the plantation. My watch pings on my wrist with directions. The wind blows against my body, and I take in the area around me. The rolling hills and green grassy fields behind the white fence posts are mesmerizing. The properties out here are bigger. I come to the final turnoff and progress up the hickory tree-lined drive to the large house. White pillars surround the first floor and the balcony on the second level. The driveway curves into a wide circle. Several motorcycles are off to the side. I park my bike amongst them. I look at them, trying to see if I see the affiliation but can't see any.

With my backpack over my shoulder and my saddlebags over the other, I move toward the door. Before I get to it, it swings open, and there stands Snake. He's not an ugly guy, but something about him turns me off. The other night at the bar, he was checking me out, and it gave me the creeps. His brown hair is styled short and brushed back in an almost perfect quaff. His body is trim and compact. He's dressed in black slacks and a bright-blue shirt that is open at the collar. He moves down the wide stairs toward me. As he approaches, I realize the other thing that turns me off about him is he's the same height as me—five foot nine. That means in heels I'll stand over him. I like men who are taller than I am. Reaper. I shake that thought from my mind and hold out my hand to shake his.

"River, you're here finally." He pushes my hand to the side and pulls me into his body. I hold stiff, confused. I didn't give him my name or permission to call me that. I also don't want to hug him. I struggle and pull back.

"Snake." I purse my lips after I say his name.

"Come, darling, our room is ready for you." He reaches for my hand. When I twist it away, he grabs my wrist and tightly grips it. He pulls me to the entrance, and I step from the bright light to the dark interior of his home.

The house has a coldness to it, and I shiver. I can't control the reaction because I feel the evil in this place. I twist my arm to break his grip and hug my arms over my chest against my bags. A fine dusting of gooseflesh pops up on my body as I look around me. The interior is done in dark, rich colors. To my left is the formal dining room and to the right are the open doors into the library. The sweeping staircase in front of me is the center piece. Pictures of what must be family members line the walls. Some of the people are in Civil War regalia. I'm shocked that the house hasn't been updated.

"Oh, don't mind the place. I bought it like this and just kept it the same." He chuckles. "Let me show you our suite so you can change and get comfortable." His choice of words hit me.

"I'm not staying with you." I step back toward the door as the feeling of being trapped hits me.

FOUR

REAPER

I WATCH as Jinx takes off on her bike. I want to stop her, but I can't jeopardize my case for her. My cell rings, and I look down to see an unknown number. I hate that when I'm under I have to be careful who I talk to and where. I look at the farmer who offered to drive me out to Snake's plantation.

"Yeah," I grumble into the phone.

"Chatter is that he's got a new lady love and she's a Maiden. Said something about sealing the deal this weekend," Anderson says before he hangs up.

I grip the phone so tight it starts to crumble in my hand. I release my hold and need to get myself under control. I know who the reference is in regard to, and over my dead body will he claim her.

"So, the old plantation you're going to has been bought by a Northerner," the farmer supplies. "They have parties there every weekend. Guys similar to you have been in and out of there. You're not like them though. They are bad; you are not so much. They don't care about others, and the number of girls that have been disappearing from the area makes some of us think it has something to do with this Snake and his guys. But the sheriff won't do anything about him. It's a shame to see that old plantation being destroyed this way. The family that built it had so much bad luck, but they stuck with it for as long as they could. When their sons were all killed in the war, it fell into disrepair. One of the daughters fought to keep it together. When she passed, one of her grandsons held on to it through the Depression and so much more. Just recently, however, another turn of bad luck hit the family, and the property was sold at auction to this Jorgenson man. He's brought an element to the countryside we've never had here before. They wear cuts similar to yours that say Defiance on them too but not with a dragon."

His words give me pause, and I turn to look at him. My eyes flare wide. "Hell's Defiance?"

"Yeah, that's it." He turns for the road, and I see the fear in his eyes at my tone.

Fuck, my girl is in more danger than she knows. As he turns down the long driveway, I pray I get there on time.

"I don't know who you are, kid, but I know a good guy when I see one. If you need anything, let me know." He slides a card in my direction, and I look back at him after I take it in. "Yeah, I'm that." He smiles.

I pocket the card in the interior pocket of my leather jacket and hop out when he stops the truck. I grab my saddle bags out of the back and sling them over my shoulder. I want to question him about what he knows, but the card confirmed everything.

"Thanks for the ride, sir. I hope I don't have to be in touch."

"You need all the luck you can get if rumors are true that your girl found the brooch," he says with a chuckle, and I slam the door, unsure of what he means.

I move up the stairs and knock on the door. No one answers, but I hear raised voices. One of them being Jinx's. I open the door and she whips around.

"I told you, you either stay with me or it's no deal," Snake says with a level of evil in his voice that I've only heard a few times in my life.

Jinx sees me and for a moment I see fear in her eyes, but then it turns to relief. She runs for me and jumps in my arms. I take her and all of her bags in my arms. My hands grip her ass.

"I tried to keep our secret that we were a couple, but he's insisting I stay with him. In *his* room." She looks into my eyes, and I see her silent plea.

Well, fuck.

I pull her head down and just before I take her lips, I growl, "You're mine, baby girl." I kiss her like I've wanted to for days. I take everything she has and more. My tongue sweeps in and dominates her mouth. Her arms wrap around my neck, and her fingers are in my hair. I move a hand from her luscious ass to her thick hair and yank her head where I want it. Taking the kiss even deeper.

"Okay, that's enough," Snake yells, and I don't stop because I'm not on his time.

When I pull away, her eyes are glassed over with desire. "I got you," I whisper, and she tightens around me, remembering where we are.

"She's my girl, Snake, and I don't share," I say as I set her next to me. I grab her bags and take them in one hand while the other curls around her shoulders and pulls her into my body. She fits perfectly, her curves blending with my hardness. I want to feel all of her, but I need to get my head in this game.

"Why didn't you tell me?" Snake moves toward us, and I watch as his eyes continue to rove over her body.

"Eyes here, fucker." I point to my eyes, and he flips his toward me. The coldness in them causes Jinx to shiver, and I pull her in tighter. "Jinx and I didn't want our clubs to know yet. It's been a fast and deep relationship. If there is an issue, we can go to town to stay."

"No, we have a celebration tonight for her. I'll have the contract ready for you both on Tuesday." His head tilts with a slight turn, and his eyes crinkle slightly. "If your clubs didn't know, isn't this a breach of their trust?"

"I told my club," Jinx says quickly, and I wonder how we're going to play this off if he calls and questions them.

"She'll stay with me in my room." I'm not letting her out of my sight. Not with everything that's really going on here. I still need to tell her.

He nods, and a woman in a white-and-black uniform moves toward us. She leads us to a room on the second floor at the back of the house. It has an en-suite bathroom. After the door is closed, Jinx swings around and starts to talk, but I hold a finger up to my lips. I don't trust Snake. It could show a bit of my hand, but I pull out my phone and open the app that will detect bugs and other electronic devices in the room. I find a couple and then switch to another app that will distort sound. I move toward her, and she doesn't backtrack, for which I'm glad. I pull her into my arms and drop my head next to her ear. To the camera I found, it will look like I'm continuing the show we started downstairs. To help, I let my hands roam her body and pray I'm strong enough to keep this decent.

"Don't look when I tell you, but there is a camera in the picture over the fireplace. There's also some listening devices by the bed and in the bathroom." She pulls away, her eyes flaring wide. I pull her back and bury her face in my neck. Her teeth scrape my skin, and my cock jumps between us. "I'll protect you," I growl before I yank her head back and take her lips in another deep kiss. I'm pushing her, and I don't care. I pull away slightly so I can get her jacket off. I need her under me for several reasons. For the viewer's pleasure and so I can touch her more.

She moans as I feel her working my jacket and then shirt. I pull away and rip my shirt over my head, and she stares at me before she does the same. Her breasts are almost spilling out of her black lacy bra. I can make out her nipple piercings. Tattoos line her body in a swirl of colors and black ink. I drink in everything about her and push her onto the bed. I'm over her in an instant. My legs tangle with hers, and my hand goes to her neck, where I squeeze slightly. Her head tips back and her eyes go half-mast.

"Have you ever done breath play?" I whisper in her ear as I lean over her. My interrupter will distort our words, but I bet Snake will come check out what's going on soon enough. I only have so much time.

"No. But I've wanted to." Her eyes flick down, and I squeeze a little tighter, letting her know I'm game.

My fingers itch to do so much more to her. She laces one hand around my bicep and the other at my waist, her little nails digging in. I shift my hand from her throat to her chin, and she sighs.

I need to get under control, but the people watching will want to know why we didn't continue. I shift her more up on the bed and put her head on the pillows then return to my position between her thighs. Her legs wrap around me and pull me in tight.

"You are in danger," I say softly as I nibble on her neck. I move to her ear. "Hell's Defiance is here. Do you have any enemies with them? Other than Phantom?" Her body tightens, and her legs start to loosen from around me. I grab them and hold her in place. "Remember they are watching." Her body instantly changes. Her eyes lose their passion, and I hate that I did that to her. I took it away. I want it back, but I have to figure out a plan. "Don't back away now, River." Using her real name stops her, and those beautiful gray-blue eyes flare wide again. The storm brewing in them almost pulls me in. I see the darker ring around the outer edge that you only see when you are this close to her. "Dig those nails into my back so they think we are doing something." She starts to nod, but my grip on her chin stops her movement. She slowly blinks, then I feel her nails drag along my side. I throw my head back in an exaggeration of desire. "Do you?" I ask again, referring to any enemies within Hell's Defiance, and she nods.

"Stanley has a brother. In court he threatened to kill us both," she says softly.

"I swear I'll protect you." This time when I take her lips, it's a sip. Then a longer sip before I plunge in. Her lips are swollen and bruised from all my previous kisses, but this one is real and not for show. She feels it too and her fingers flex into my skin. When I pull back, she has that low-lidded desire look in her eyes again. "With everything," I swear, and I mean it. I'll do everything I can to protect her. A plan starts to form in my mind, but it'll be a last-ditch effort if needed.

RIVER

I HATE that I have to do this, and I worry that I've put Reaper in more danger. I can't text Scout to tell her what's going on because there is a jammer somewhere in this huge house. Both Reaper and my phones no longer have a signal. I even tried email, and I can't do that either.

A guard came up while we were making out on the bed and demanded to check our room. Reaper later told me about the signal jammer on his phone, but after that the thing stopped working. We have to come up with other ways to talk without being heard.

Now I'm standing here in front of the mirror in an outfit I was told I had to wear, courtesy of our host. I hate it, but I have no choice. Reaper says he'll try to figure out a way to get us out of here. I need to find out if Snake has any of the girls here and then I'm out. I look at the skintight leather leggings and cropped lace-up leather tank.

"I don't understand why I have to wear this?"

Reaper is wearing his jeans along with a black T-shirt and his cut. He still gets to wear his knife, but I have to wear this outfit that makes me feel like an object. I can't even wear a bra with it. I've worn things like this before, but it was my choice when I did.

"You look sexy as fuck," Reaper says as his eyes roam up and down my body. I look at him in the mirror and see the desire in his eyes. He wants me, but he's also just playing along to protect me. The thought that Smith is here scares me. Scout barely survived Stanley, and I was knocked unconscious when I tried to stop him. If Brazen hadn't come in when she did with Vixen, we'd both be dead right now. My body shivers at the thought that I may never see my family again. Before this moment, I took them for granted. I didn't value them as much as I should.

Reaper must sense my fear because he leans into me, and I look up into the mirror at him. His big, tattooed, hot as fuck body is pressed against my back. I try to hide the tears in my eyes, but he spins me and lifts me to the counter. He presses between my thighs, and I feel his hard cock against my core. He can't fake that.

"I told you I'd protect you. Don't go there," he growls in my ear before he drags his teeth down my carotid artery. My body lights up as the door to the room is opened.

"Master Jorgenson wants you to come downstairs," the woman says. He treats her like a slave, and she keeps her eyes dropped to the floor.

Reaper pulls me from the counter before he leans forward again. "We need a door that fucking locks."

I hide my smile and nod slightly.

He takes my hand and moves me out of the bathroom and into the main room. The heels I'm in are tall and skinny. They click against the hardwood floor as Reaper's long legs eat up the distance. When we are out the door, he keeps a hold of me as we are led downstairs to the formal dining room I saw earlier. There is Snake sitting at the head of the table, and to his right is Elias Smith. I've only seen him in court. He's with Hell's Defiance MC in Texas, not here like Stanley was. His open stare of hate falls on me and I feel Reaper tense. His hand lands on my leather clad ass and holds me tight to his body. Other men sit at the table. There are only two open seats, and they aren't together. The one to Snake's left and one at this end.

FIVE

REAPER

WE'RE SO FUCKED. There is no fucking way I can have her sit that far away from me. She's not leaving my side as long as Smith is sitting there. Plus, Snake has made it clear he wants her too.

I look around the room and make the only decision I can. I take the empty chair far from Snake and pull River onto my lap. I lay my claim in that moment again.

"Fine," Snake says. "Shift, everyone."

Everyone shifts down a chair. I slide into the next one and put River in the chair I just vacated so she is further from both men. I pull her chair close to mine.

"Hello, Jinx," Smith says, and he smiles at her.

His grin is wide and reminds me of the Joker. "I'm Crazy, just in case you didn't know. My brother is Phantom." He rises from his seat, and I get to my feet and stand in front of River to keep her out of his sight. "You're a jumpy fucker. Snake, tell him to leave, and we can start our conversation with her."

"Crazy, sit down, this is my place," Snake orders, and Smith sits down. I wait until I don't feel the threat anymore before I sit too.

Dinner is strained and I notice that Jinx barely eats. I lean into her body and whisper to her, "Eat, baby girl, please." She nods and takes a bite of the meat.

"What are you whispering about?" Snake asks, and I don't miss a beat.

"I told her to eat so she has strength for what I'm going to do to her later." The table erupts in laughter, and her thigh flexes under my hand. I've tried to keep a hand on her or an arm around her through this whole play for power from Snake.

As soon as dinner is done, the table is cleared and Snake leads us through the library into a billiard room. There is a bar set up and several young girls are present. They are skimpily dressed in barely there, see-through clothes. I feel Jinx's body tighten and she pauses. I push her forward with my arm around her and move to a large chair, where I take a seat and pull her down on my knee.

My hand is possessively wrapped around her waist, holding her tight. When I flex my fingers against her warm skin, she looks away from the girls to Snake. She relaxes and leans back into my body. My hand splays against her belly, and I roll her belly button piercing between my knuckles.

"You have a problem with the entertainment?" Smith says as he walks by us. "Maybe you should show us some of those moves you have."

My hand tightens as her body goes ramrod straight. He chuckles, and she bristles even more. I turn her head away from him and kiss her deep until she softens. I lean into her ear.

"Not right now," I whisper so only she can hear me over the loud rock music.

When she pulls away, her eyes are wide and she's taking me in. I made sure at dinner she only drank water from a pitcher that was served to everyone or from a fresh and sealed bottle. I have a feeling Snake's up to something.

"Get us a drink." I point to the barrel of ice with long necks by the bar. She nods and stands up. I watch her like a hawk as she moves across the room. My next words are for Snake.

"She's mine. I said it numerous times. You won't fuck with her," I say with an edge of a bite.

Jinx works through the crowd and grabs the long necks when she reaches the bar. A girl screams, and we both turn. I take my eyes off Jinx for only a moment. When I turn back, a man with Smith has her in his arms. I'm up and across the room in an instant.

"Take your hands off my woman," I bark at the rider as he gropes her ass.

She grabs his hand and twists as she bends it backward, taking him to his knees. He comes up and is ready to hit her. I have my gun out of my back holster and at his chin. Everything is quiet around us as the music stops and people still. I hold out my hand to Jinx, and she curls behind me as I refocus on the room.

"I told you to take your hands off her. You hit her or threaten to hit her, and I'll kill you." This goes against my badge but not my nature. She is mine, and I will kill for her. I wrap my arm around her and hold her tighter.

Snake laughs and claps his hands. "Enough," he says, and all the bikers step back. He's not affiliated with an MC, but I missed something about him. I secure my gun at my back again and face him. "If she's yours, why doesn't she have a property patch?" he asks, and I realize I played into his hand. She was told she couldn't wear her cut with her outfit, and I couldn't figure out why until right this moment. He was testing us. But little does he know. I slip off my cut and turn to her. She looks up at me and shakes her head, but I stop it with a look. She's freaked out, and I know why. I slip the cut onto her body and turn back to Snake. Crazy is now standing next to him.

"Better?"

Crazy's face is pinched. His lips thin as his anger grows. But Snake isn't fazed at all. I watch as he raises his hands to chest level again and claps. It's a slow golf clap filled with sarcasm, and I feel the hair on the back of my neck rise. When he stops, he looks at her and then at me.

"If she's yours, you'll marry her tomorrow. If not, she'll be warming my bed and then Crazy's before he takes his revenge on her."

Everything in my body stills. I hear the cocking of a gun, and Jinx and I both turn. Standing in the doorway is the butler who's been directing the servants tonight. He has a shotgun aimed at Jinx and me.

Everything is moving too fast, and I can't catch up. I'm not sure how I'll get us out of this.

SIX

JINX

I LOOK AT THE GIRLS. Some are barely eighteen. They are drugged out and don't realize what's going on. The reason the one screamed is because she was lifted onto a table and told to strip. When she didn't do it fast enough, the guys pulled her down and yanked her top off. I'm fucking scared. My palms are sweating, and my breathing is tight.

When Reaper put his cut on me, I knew it wasn't the right thing to do. He doesn't want to be strapped down to me. He was only helping me out. I have to stop this and escape before my luck turns worse. There are several pictures of the brooch in this room. I'm freaking out because I was able to get out the book and read it a bit earlier.

The brooch had been cursed by an Irish Druid priestess before the family came to the Americas. One of the sons had fallen in love with her, but his family wanted him to have a better match. He broke off the engagement, and she returned the brooch he'd given her, but not before placing a curse on it. According to the book, love would be hard for the barrier of it. But those who threw it away or disregarded it would be cursed with bad luck. Ever since Reaper tried to get rid of it, he's had bad luck. Now he has the worse luck. I've had good luck until I walked into this house. There has to be something about that brooch and this house other than I think the previous owners of it were related to the man who broke the priestess's heart.

I move from my position behind Reaper. I can't let him do this. I want to marry a strong man who loves me for me. Not someone who is forced to marry me. I'm not going to sleep with Snake. I'll leave.

"I have a better deal," I say as I move in front of Reaper.

"Hush," he demands, and I ignore him. Something in me wants to listen to what he has to say, but something deep down wants to protect him.

He's done nothing but be completely honest and protected me.

"Instead, I won't race for you. I'll not race at all this next season. Get another rider. If I'm not in the race, they'll have a better chance to win. Bet and win. As for Crazy…" I scoff at the name. It fits him. Like Stanley, he has blond hair and blue eyes. He's a boy next door kind of cute except for the evil look in his eyes and the tattoos. If I didn't know any better, I would think I was standing in front of a Brad Pitt look-alike, but I do know better. "As for him." I pause again. Reaper isn't going to like this. His hands flex around my waist. "I'll fight him. Three rounds of five minutes." I know I can beat him if I get him to the ground, but I'm not sure what he's trained in.

"Fuck no," Reaper says, and I ignore him again.

Ever so slowly, the sides of Snake's lips tip up into a smile. Crazy has a huge grin on his face.

"Right now," Crazy says as he high-fives one of his guys.

"Not fucking happening. You have to respect her 'cause she's mine." Reaper lifts the shoulder of his cut that I still have on.

"I have a counteroffer. You fight one of the rounds and Reaper fights the other two. But he will still marry you tomorrow, or you'll be in my bed." Snake rubs his chin. "I planned to have you there for a long time, but now I'll settle for one night. I'm not going to give that up for anything other than you being married to another man. I'd even consider killing Reaper to have you, but that could muck up a lot of my plans."

"I want her." Crazy moves toward Snake. "Not Reaper. He had nothing to do with my brother. She did that."

"She's a woman. What are you going to do?" Snake looks at Crazy in disgust over the fact that he wants to punch me around. Snake wants to rape me, so they are both the same in my book.

"To your room. You'll fight tomorrow, and the wedding will be in the evening." Several men surround us and direct us upstairs. These aren't bikers. These guys look like mercenaries.

We are pushed into the room, and the door is locked from the outside. I move to the windows and find a gate is pulled down over them now. We can't get out across the balcony. We are well and fully trapped.

"Fuck," Reaper exclaims as he throws something. I turn to see his Bowie knife impaled in the picture and the lens of a camera shattered. "What the fuck were you thinking, River?" He advances on me, and I back up. He doesn't scare me, but I can tell he's upset, and I don't know what he plans to do next.

"I had to save you. I'm not going to have you marry me out of pity," I yell back at him.

REAPER

I TAKE in her words for a moment.

Pity.

I have no such thought of that when it comes to her. I want her. I need to protect her, and I only have so many options. The plan becomes crystal clear in my mind. If I marry her, I can kill both of them and she can't testify against me. I can save her from sleeping with Snake. I can have her as mine.

I need to get her out of this fucking town.

She starts pacing, and I watch her as she moves. I haven't responded yet, but I can imagine in her mind she thinks I'm agreeing with her.

I move and stand in front of her, stopping her pacing. I grab the hand that she has up by her mouth as she nibbles on her fingernail. I'm sure she's trying to figure a way out of everything we've got ourselves into.

I press her hand against my jean-clad cock.

"Does that feel like pity? I want you. Fuck, I

want you so much I'm willing to fuck over everything else just to have you. If marrying you is the only way I can save you, then I'll fucking do that." Her hand flexes and my cock turns to steel. She looks up at me and I see the desire in her eyes. I've taken care of the camera, but there are still sound devices in the room. I know they heard us. But right now, I don't care. I need her.

"On your fucking knees, River." I use her real name and she drops down. "Your sexy, curvy body has been calling to me all fucking night, and I'm going to get a taste before we are married." I unbuckle my belt and unsnap my jeans. She's looking up at me with her full lips puffy from my kisses. Her eyes are big and round, and her pupils are dilated. I won't force her though. Right before I lower my zipper, I really look at her. I see things I know others have never seen. Her fear. Her need. "Tell me what you want," I order her.

"I want you. If it's just this night, I want it. If it's only this, I need you. I need you to order me around and do all the things I crave."

"You crave me, baby girl." I use the nickname I've given her.

"Yes, Master," she says so softly that I read her lips and not hear her words.

I reach down and rub her cheek. She's so soft.

Her skin is flushed, and I'm only thinking about her.

"Take it out and suck it like it's your Popsicle, baby," I tell her, and she reaches up for my zipper. She slowly drags it down, and when she opens my fly, my cock is pressing against my boxers. She pulls my jeans down and then grabs the edge of my boxers. My cock springs free in her face, and she leans forward to lick off the precum oozing from the tip. Her lips wrap around the head of my cock, and I can't look away as I watch her mouth slide down my length. She takes me deep into her throat and swallows slowly. My head falls back on my shoulders, and I moan as she slides back and then takes me deep again. "You like that, baby girl. You want me to come in your throat or your tight cunt?" I grip her hair and hold her head, stopping the next slide. She's only moved over me twice and I'm ready to blow for her. I've wanted her for days, and it's been so long for me.

"My cunt." She doesn't cringe at the word as she releases my cock.

"Show your man what you got." I step back and start stripping, but I watch her more, not caring about my clothes. She reaches for the laces on her top when I get a better idea. "Wait," I order her, and she drops her hands. I see her moment of hesitation, and I move naked across the room to where my Bowie is still impaled in the camera. I pull out my knife and rip the camera from the wall, dragging the wires out to cut them. I move back to her and stand in front of her. She's breathtaking in her silent beauty. Her long curly hair hangs down her back. Her lips are swollen, and her lipstick is smudged. I look down and see the red coloring on my cock, and my hold on my control snaps.

I grip the front of her top and cut the leather laces. Her full C-cup breasts pop free. They are firm with rosy nipples that are erect and begging for my mouth. I don't want to cut her, so I nod at the pants.

"You do that part." I wave my knife at the skintight leggings.

She unzips them and shimmies them off her wide hips. She turns, giving me her back as she reaches down with one hand to pull the tight cuff from her ankle. She's bent over and her ass is in the air. I drop to my knees and drive my knife into the floor. I grip her thighs and pull her back to my face. I lick her from her clit to her cunt. She moans and my grip tightens as I get my first taste of her.

The need to be here always overtakes me, and I continue to lick her over and over before I stiffen my tongue and fuck her. My cock oozes more precum and I stand. One hand holds her in the bent over position and the other grips her hip as I slowly press into her tightness.

"Fuck, you're so tight, babe," I groan, and she cries out as I bottom out inside her. She is shaking her head, moving around, her hair brushing along the floor. I hold myself inside of her, waiting for her to catch her breath.

"Fuck me, Master," she finally says, and I pull out and slam back in. This time I hold both of her hips tight. My fingers dig into her flesh, and the bite of pain causes her to cry out. I move in and out of her a few more times before letting her stand up. I pull out and look down to see my cock is covered in her, which puts me on edge even more.

"Bed. On your back," I order her again, and she doesn't disappoint.

She lies down and opens her legs to me, giving me a prime view of her pink pussy. I crawl up the bed and grab her leg. I throw it over my shoulder as I slam into her and then I take her neck in a grip. I squeeze and her pupils dilate. The color almost gone with her desire. She moans, and I start moving over and over inside of her as I take her air and then give it back. Every time I release her neck, she gushes all over my cock.

I let go of her neck and roll us. She sits up and proceeds to ride me. I grip her hips and slide my hands up to her breasts. I pull on her nipple piercings and she throws her head back. Her long hair falls down her back to my legs. She rides me hard, and I'm getting close. I need her to come first. I reach between her legs and pinch her clit. She screams my name, my real name, as she comes hard. Her pussy milks my cock, and I flex inside her a couple of times before I sit up and lift her up and down on my cock until I finally come deep inside her.

"River," I groan her name as my cum coats her insides. She falls to my chest and kisses my pec, right over my heart.

"Don't worry, I'm on birth control," she says, and I hold her tighter.

"We'll talk in the shower." For one second, I think of how much I wanted her to say she wasn't on birth control. That she could get pregnant with my baby. It's a sobering thought.

I have to get us out of here and away from Snake and Crazy. I have to get out so I can be with her. She is not a one-weekend fuck.

She's my forever.

SEVEN

RIVER

I SLIDE my leg to the side and feel the coolness of the sheets. I push up and brush my hair from my face. I'm on my stomach in the room Snake put us in yesterday. I look around and see Reaper sitting in a chair watching me. He's shirtless and has his long arms folded across his chest, his head cocked to the side. His tattooed brow raised as he watches me. I turn around and pull the sheet up to cover my breasts. He shakes his head and instantly I want him again.

We fucked so many times last night, you'd think he was done with me, but he's not. I see his cock harden behind his jeans and chuckle as I shake my head at him. I slide to the edge of the bed and grab the sheet as I walk to him with it clouding around my body. I straddle his lap and rest my pussy right over his jean-clad cock.

I lean forward and lay my head on his chest. I'm about to rear up and ask him if I can ride again when the lock disengages from the door. Reaper is up so fast with me behind him and his gun aimed at the door.

The reality of our situation hits me like a ton of bricks. I look around his body as the maid comes in again. She has a large garment bag with her. She moves to the bathroom and hangs it up.

"Master would like you to dress and come down to breakfast."

She walks out. Reaper turns to look at me.

"River, we need to get out of here. But don't fight Crazy." He holds on to my face. His fingers bury in my hair, and I look back up at him.

"I can hold him off—"

"I don't trust him." He interrupts me. "He'll fight dirty."

"Okay." I drop my eyes, but he lifts my chin and forces me to look at him.

"I swear we'll make it out of here."

"I know." If I've learned anything in the last couple of days, it's that Klay is a man of his word.

He turns me around. "Go get dressed, baby."

He smacks my ass and sends me toward the bathroom.

The garment bag is calling me. I can't stop myself. I unzip it and look inside.

"Motherfucker," I exclaim, and Reaper is right there by my side, gun drawn, looking for danger.

"Yeah." He turns away and starts to walk out when I point to the dress.

"Wait. You're not freaked out by this?" The sheet falls from my body and I'm standing naked in front of him.

"Nope. I picked it out."

"You what?" My hands land on my hips and I square off against him.

"The maid came up earlier and said her master told us to pick a dress. I didn't want to wake you, so I picked this one. Thought it would fit you the best."

I look back at the dress. He's right. It's what I would have picked if I were really getting married.

"You're not upset about this? I am."

He shakes his head. "This is what I need to do to protect you." He moves closer to me and pulls me into his body. When he leans down, he whispers in my ear, "There is so much more going on here than just Snake forcing me to prove you're mine. If this is how I protect you, then that's what

I'll do." He kisses the top of my head and moves to leave.

"I want the man I marry to be in love with me." I stomp my foot.

He stops and turns to look at me again, then he's on me in the next moment. I don't know how a man as big as him moves so fast. He's got me lifted up and in his arms. He sits me on the counter and steps into my body, spreading my legs.

"What makes you think I don't love you?"

I scoff, and he grips my chin tight.

"The moment I saw you, I knew you'd change my life. I haven't fucked a woman in a long time, but you I wanted instantly. One day I'll explain more to you, but right now you'll marry me and I'll make you safe. I'll love you, and you'll figure it out and fall for me too." He kisses me deep, his tongue pushing its way into my mouth, and he takes my breath away. My eyes flutter closed. My hands pull him into my body more and my toes curl.

I know I'm falling for him. I know that he's right, but I don't want it to be like this.

He pulls away and walks out of the bathroom, leaving me needy and flushed for him. I jump down and take a quick shower. I style my hair in a thick braid down my back and dress in jeans, a tank top, and a flannel shirt with the sleeves rolled up. I slip on my socks and boots before moving out to the main room.

I watch him as he works on his phone and realize he's texting.

"Our phones are working!" I move to mine.

"No, I'm reading something I downloaded to my phone before." He stops to look at me. His lips tip up ever so slightly and my stomach drops. Yep, I'm in love with him. But I'm scared that he'll just walk away when we get out of this situation.

He moves to me and takes my hand to lead me from the room. The maid left the door unlocked so we could head to the dining room.

REAPER

I FEEL like I've known her forever instead of only a few days. When she caught me on my phone, I almost told her the truth, but I couldn't. Our phones are still blocked, but I had downloaded files on Snake and Smith. I was reading the things I hadn't from before on them. I need to find a way out of this for her.

I knew I was in love with her the moment I told

my career to go to hell. The moment I didn't escape immediately and get to where I could call in the calvary. I wasn't going to leave her, and now she's protected by my badge too.

Or she will be.

We turn the corner into the dining room. I expect it to be full just like the night before, but only Snake sits there at the head. I move to sit next to him and put her on my other side so she isn't close to him. I'm going to keep her as far from him as I can.

"Let's call a truce," he says, and the maid pours me a cup of coffee along with River.

"Let us go."

"I can't. Crazy wants his revenge." He pauses for a moment, and I can almost see the cogs in his head moving. "River would be safe if you gave her to me and left."

"No."

"Fine. Your wedding will be at sunset on the patio out back by the pool."

"Okay."

We eat a quiet meal. He doesn't try to make any more conversation with us, and I'm still trying to figure out how I can get her out of here. I know he's going to make her a widow as soon as he can so he can have her himself.

We end up back in our room, and I type out a

OFF BALANCE 75

text and push send. As soon as we get away from the signal blockers, it will deliver and I can get a team out here to save us. I keep the message short and simple.

ME:

> Compromised. Need extraction for myself plus one.

Promptly at four, Snake's guards come and get me from the room. The maid follows behind them to start getting River ready. I wanted to kiss her goodbye, but the guards grabbed my arms. I didn't want to fight and cause her more stress. She's been pacing the room or sketching in a pad she had in her pack. I've also caught her reading a journal she told me the historical society gave her about the brooch. She hasn't told me much about it, and I'm starting to get curious.

An hour later, I'm standing by a man I don't recognize but imagine is a priest by his collar and staunch appearance. We face the entrance as Snake walks out with my girl on his arm.

Her long hair is mostly up with a few curls hanging down like a halo. She has a flower crown on her head, and she's wearing the dress I picked out. The simple sheath hugs all her curves and is a pure white that makes her tan skin glow. Her arms and back are exposed. The collar of the dress comes up to her collarbone and wraps around her delicate throat. I can see my handprints on her skin from when I took her last night. It's a heady feeling knowing she's mine now. She moves on dainty white heels toward me with only a slight train.

EIGHT

RIVER

I'M STANDING in the living room of this plantation house with Klay's arm around my waist. He's in a black suit and looks hotter than I've ever seen him. He's my husband now. I only wanted to get married once, and here I am married to a man who says he loves me. But we barely know each other. He's got a huge grin on his face as if this is all real. We can have this annulled as soon as we get out of here. I can't divorce him. That I won't do. Daddy always said marriage was for life, and I plan to do that.

Snake giving me away made me realize how fake this all was. Watching Crazy sitting there shaking in his chair because he wanted to hurt me was what I needed to remember I was doing this to save Klay's life.

My husband.

I think about the journal. How the priestess wanted only to love, but it was ripped from her. The curse lasts until a true love claims the gem. I need to give it to someone else because this isn't true love. I want it to be. I want him to really love me.

I'm so lost in my head that I don't realize everyone is staring at me until Klay's arm tightens around my body. I look up as Crazy comes running into the room with a gun in his hand. The man truly has a few loose screws. He shoots and plaster from the ceiling comes raining down. Klay pulls a gun from behind his back and fires. I watch as blood blooms from Crazy's forehead.

Guns cock and point at us.

"I'll call the sheriff and get this taken care of as soon as possible," Snake says. "Go upstairs," he orders Klay and me.

We move toward the stairs together, and I'm freaked out. I don't know what's going to happen now.

"On second thought, I'll give you tonight," Snake shouts behind us. "Make it worth her while, Reaper. Pretty soon she'll be warming my bed." He chuckles.

As soon as we're back in our room and the door closes, I spin around to face him.

"Why did you kill him?"

"He was going to shoot you next." He shrugs like it was nothing to take a life. "I told you I would protect you."

"Klay, you can't just shoot everyone who threatens me. Now you're going to jail, and I'm going to have to sleep with Snake."

"The fuck you say." He advances on me and spins me around. He releases the collar of my dress and then lowers the zipper at the base of my spine. The dress falls in a pool at my feet. "I won't let that happen. Help will be here by morning," he says and lifts me up into his arms. He lays me on the bed, and I watch as he strips himself. My heart clenches in my throat as I'm sure I'm falling for him deeply. He could break me, and he has no clue.

When he settles himself between my legs, I wrap my legs around his hips, cradling him to me. He holds my face between his big, tattooed hands.

"I'm going to get you out of here. I'll make you safe, just like I did down there. No one threatens my wife," he says before he kisses me deeply.

His tongue slides against mine, and my hands wrap around his shoulders. When he finally pulls away from my lips, he trails kisses down my neck to my chest, then my breasts. He takes one nipple in his mouth and sucks it deep. I squirm from the desire he's pulling from me. If this is the last night I get him, I'll make it worth everything for him.

We make love slowly and long into the night. I'm wrapped in his arms as we fall asleep. I wait until I hear him snoring before sharing my thoughts.

"I can't divorce you. I'm sure I love you," I say softly, and then I fall asleep too.

KLAY

I HEAR her as she tells me she loves me, and it takes every bit of my training to keep from responding. I do love her. In the short time I've known her, I've fallen for her. I hold her tight, praying that my phone was right when it said my message was delivered.

I only have to keep her safe until they get here, then we'll get out of here and I'll keep her as mine. I'll have to tell her about my job eventually, but I'm going to hold on to that secret for a bit longer because I don't want to freak her out.

The next morning the sun wakes me up as it

rises, and I move to the chair and watch her like I did the day before. I need to get as much of her as I can because I know the job will pull me away from her for a bit. I'm going to miss her, and I hope she doesn't run from me like I fear she will. I see the brooch sitting on the side table and pick it up. I roll it in my hand and still think it's costume jewelry. She told me some of the story about it.

I don't know if I believe in curses or not, but something deep inside me urges me to make a plea to the priestess who enchanted it.

"Keep her safe and keep her as mine. I love her." I whisper the words and set the brooch back down as River wakes up.

"It's time, isn't it?" she asks me, and I see the worry etched on her beautiful face.

I sit on the bed and drag her naked body across mine.

"I'm going to make you safe," I say against her ear, keeping my voice low so the listening devices don't pick up what I'm about to tell her next. "I got a text message out yesterday. Help will be coming soon."

I don't tell her it's the ATF. I don't tell her the truth she should hear. Instead, I kiss her and send her to get ready.

She dresses in black jeans with her boots, a white tank top, and another flannel tied at the waist. She slips her cut on before we head downstairs. We are dressed similarly, and she holds on to my hand as if she's afraid I'll be taken from her.

When we turn into the dining room, Snake is sitting there with two folders in front of him. That sixth sense I've always used starts screaming at me. Something isn't right.

"Have a seat," Snake orders, and I look around, expecting a trap.

"Wait," River says. When I look at her, she shakes her head. "I need to call home." She's trying to come up with a plan too, but we are at the end, and I know it.

"You can't until after the meeting." Snake takes a bite of his breakfast and watches her.

We sit down and again are served coffee. It's like *Groundhog Day*. Everything is so similar to yesterday except this conversation.

"Is there a point to the meeting anymore?" She takes a sip of her coffee and waits to see if he'll answer her question. "I mean, look, I'm not racing for you. I promised I wouldn't race at all to save Reaper."

"That's so sweet of you. Crazy was ready to kill him until I stopped him. But at last, Crazy has left us." He acts like Smith just got up and left and didn't die on his hardwood floor from my bullet.

She huffs. "When are you going to let us go?"

"After I get you." Everything locks up in my body.

"What!" She jumps up, pushing her chair back.

"Sit down, Ms. Schmidt, or should I say Mrs. Ulrich?" I turn to look at him. "Yes, Mr. Ulrich, I know all about you. I *know*." He flicks his hand toward the two folders in front of him. My gut rolls and I push away from the table. I grab River's hand and drag her to the door, but two guards appear. I pull my gun and press it into one of their faces. He steps back, and I open the door. Out front is not only the sheriff's vehicle but all of Snake's and Smith's men are there too.

I turn back to look at her. "I love you," I mouth the words and walk out the door, dragging her along with me. She doesn't pause. We make it to the sheriff, who shakes his head at me.

"You should've notified me you were in the area." He opens the back door of the car, and I push River in before I slide in next to her. As I'm bending down, I look back to see Snake standing on the porch. He was sure I wouldn't take this route, and now that I have, I have to get the truth out before it's too late.

"River, I need to tell you something," I say as the sheriff talks to Snake and then walks around the car to get in. I lean in close and whisper the words, "I'm ATF." She gasps and rears back. Then her fist slams into my face. I grab her hand to check it and kiss it, but she ignores me. She pulls away and won't look at me as I watch her shift and pull something from the pocket of her jeans. It's the brooch. The brooch I wished on earlier and last I knew was on the bedside table.

The brooch that is cursed.

The sheriff turns around and looks at me. He's about to say something when the sunlight flashes on the gems that now sparkle. She's cleaned it up. His eyes focus on it, and he sits back so fast he hits his head on the window behind him.

He scrambles to get out of the car. He's around it and opening my door so fast that Snake just stares.

"Nope. I won't bring that thing into my precinct. No. I quit. They are all yours." He ushers us out of the vehicle. The man is tripping over himself to get off the property, leaving us with several guns pointed at us.

River and I are standing there, and I'm at a loss as to what to do now. When my phone pings in my pocket, I know we are saved.

"You're going to want to let us go. My handler is on his way." I pull out my phone and hold it up.

"Fuck," Snake bellows as he rushes back toward the house. "Get off my property," he yells, and I grab a hold of River and push her toward the large marble fountain in the center of the driveway.

I lie on top of her as guns start going off. We are only two people, and there are at least six guns firing in our direction. I pull my backup piece and hand it to her. Snake's men left. Only Crazy's guys remain. They are hell-bent on avenging their leader I killed.

"Can you shoot?"

I watch as she clears the gun and raises it. She pulls the trigger and a guy drops. Together we start shooting until no one is left out front. Several of the guys took off running. Snake's helicopter takes off over the back of the house. He's making a run for it. I need to get River to safety before I can go after him. I rise up and we take off for her bike.

We jump on and make it off the property without getting shot at anymore. She didn't argue with me when I took her bike and she rode bitch. We can't leave with my bike still in the shop. Plus, I need to wait for the team to get here. But I need to get her to safety. I need to find out how my cover was blown.

We check into a hotel and wait until I get a call from my handler. River is resting on the bed and hasn't called Scout yet. I don't know what she's waiting for, but she hasn't said much to me. She's just reading the journal about the brooch. The city went into lockdown shortly after we got to the hotel, so there is nothing we can do for today.

We are stuck here.

I want to talk to her, to explain, but she ignores me every time I try. I move to the bathroom and jump in the shower.

NINE

RIVER

I ROLL to the side and watch him as he disappears in the bathroom. I'm being childish and should listen to him, but I'm so upset that I'm married to a liar. He should've told me. Now I'm sitting here trying to process everything. The lies. The truths. My feelings.

All of it causes my heart to break. What is he going to do now? Was I just a means to an end for him? I flop back on the bed.

Fuck.

His phone rings, and I rise up. "Your phone," I holler for him, but he doesn't come out. I know he's been waiting for an important call.

I roll off the bed and move to grab it. It stops ringing but then starts up again.

"Klay's phone," I answer.

"Who is this?" A male voice comes across the line.

"River." I don't give any other information because I don't know who this is.

"River, you're breaking the law. I can have you arrested for answering this phone," the snidey voice shouts.

"Listen here, prick. Give me a sec and I'll take the phone to him."

"I don't care. I'll throw the book at you."

I open the bathroom door and move to the shower that's billowing steam out of it. I rip open the curtain.

"Some asshole kept calling and wants to talk to you. Said he was throwing me in jail for answering your phone," I say by way of greeting as I hold out his phone.

"Hello," he says into the phone. "Sir. Yes. Okay." He doesn't have much to say at first, but I hear the other man's voice raised in anger. "You try to prosecute my wife, and I'll report this up the ladder, and I'll walk with all my information," he growls into the phone and hangs it up.

I look at him in shock. He's willing to walk away from his job to save me. I'm confused until he pulls me into his body. His lips land on mine and I open to him. I wrap my arms around him. This is us. We are good at the sex part.

"River, I love you. I'll do anything to protect you. Now take these soaked clothes off so I can fuck you properly." His voice has a gruffness to it that causes my panties to soak. He helps me undress, then he pulls me into his body and holds me for a moment as the water beats down on us. "I'm not letting you go. I didn't want to lie to you, but I had to keep quiet in the house with all the listening devices."

"I know." I look up at him. He's right. "I just thought I was nothing more than a job."

He shakes his head as he looks down at me. "River, you've been more than a job since I first saw you. I've been willing to fuck my career since that moment."

"How do we go on from here?" I ask him the million-dollar question.

"Well, you'll be my old lady and we'll go from there. I have to let my Prez know what's going on. He knows I'm ATF. You can still be a Handmaiden. We can make this work."

I nod, unable to answer because my throat is too thick with emotion. He leans down and kisses me again. Our tongues slide together, and we are lost in each other. He kisses me so deep that I feel it in my soul. When he pulls away, we are both breathless. He turns me around and bends me over. The shower is spraying my back as he slides into my body. I throw my wet hair back, and he grabs a fist full and holds my head up as he moves himself in and out of me.

"Please, Klay," I beg because he's just teasing me. His thrusts are shallow and just barely hitting that spot where I need him.

"I fucking love when you use my name. Best fucking sound in the whole world other than when you moan."

I moan long and loud, hoping to push him. He continues to tease me, giving me part of his cock and stopping short of letting me come. When he pulls out, part of me is happy until he stops me from dropping to my knees when he turns me around. I know if I can get his cock in my mouth, I can take him over and he'll lose control and finish me off.

"Stop topping from the bottom, baby girl," he tells me and spins me again. His palm connects with my wet ass, and I scream as my clit starts throbbing more intense than it was before. I moan and squeeze my legs together. He lowers to his knees and slides his tongue through my folds.

"Please, Master," I beg him as I grip his hair tight in my fists, directing him where I want him to be. He growls and the vibration causes me to rise up on my toes. I'm so close. The need to feel him completely overrides everything. The adrenaline from earlier. The thought of losing him. It all blends together, causing a storm of emotions and desires.

I close my eyes because it's all too much.

"Open them, River," he whispers in my ear, and I realize he's standing in front of me. "Don't hide from me. Show me," he demands.

I open my eyes, and the tears are there. The feelings roll through my body. He lifts me up and presses my back into the wall as he slowly enters me completely. I feel him everywhere. His eyes are boring into me.

I see it.

The love.

My throat clogs as he starts moving. A long, slow drag out, and an equally slow thrust back in parts my body to him. I lean my head back, but I keep my eyes on him. He keeps moving, not changing the speed. The moment drags on and on as I feel him squeeze my breast and tweak my nipple ring. The dam bursts. Tears rush down my face, blending with the water, and I cry out as I come hard.

"Klay," I say his name as I lose his eyes and he takes my lips. He pulls away as he comes hard.

"River."

I bury my face in his neck and hold on tight. Something feels off with this moment. Something that I can't control. I could lose him, just like I lost my parents. His job is dangerous.

"Don't leave me," I beg him as he holds me.

"I'm never letting you go."

"No, you don't get it, Klay." I pause and pull back so he can see me. "Nine years ago, my parents went away for an anniversary weekend and never came home. I don't want to lose you too."

"River, I'm not going anywhere. I want everything with you. My baby in your belly, my property patch on your back. My house with your smell. Everything. I love you."

"You have a house?" That's all I can focus on right now because everything else is too much. I look up at him and lower my lids before I say the words.

"I love you too."

KLAY

SHE FELL ASLEEP AS SOON as I dried her off and laid her down in the bed. I'm wrapped around her, trying to figure out how this is all going to work out. I construct my letter of resignation in my mind as she sleeps curled into me. When she rolls over later, I make love to her again, and I tell her about my dog and house. I know I'm going to have to prove to her every day that I want her. That I'm not leaving her. I already knew about her parents from the little research I did on her, but hearing her say it and seeing the pain in her eyes, I realized I have to prove to her I'm not going anywhere.

I fall asleep and come awake just before dawn to my phone pinging from the bathroom. I roll away, hating that I'm leaving her warm body. My morning wood would like to take her again. As soon as I take care of Anderson, I'll go make love to my wife. I know telling the division chief that I was married the way I did wasn't good, and the threat is probably going to get me written up, but I don't care.

For the first time in my life, I don't feel aimless. I have a trajectory, and it's all because of River. I have a family that I will protect now. Her and any kids we have. I can't wait until I can talk her into having a baby. But until then, I'll help her with Scout and Skyler. They need a man looking out for them too.

I look down at the message and want to shatter

the phone against the wall. My grip on it tightens and it starts to crack. I turn back to see my wife lying there so peaceful, her skin rosy from the orgasm I gave her about an hour ago.

I promised I'd protect her.

That's what I'm doing right now. If I don't walk away and end all this, she will be in danger, not just from Smith's friends but now from the government.

Quietly I dress, and before I close the door, I look at the brooch lying on the nightstand. Fucking piece of jewelry.

Fucking curse.

TEN

RIVER

I COME AWAKE as the sun shines down on my body through the open curtains. I pull the sheet up and roll. I expect to see Klay sitting in the chair staring at me as I sleep like he loves to do, but he's not there.

The room is quiet. Too quiet. I look around and don't see his boots or jeans. I don't see his guns, Bowie, or anything else. All I see are my clothes from yesterday. All my stuff is at the plantation. I can't go get it.

Using the sheet as a wrap, I move around the room. There is no sign of him. Nothing.

He wouldn't leave me. He promised. He's

getting us food. I reason with myself, but after I dress, and he still isn't back, I know it was all a lie.

I hold myself together and move out of the room to the front desk.

"The town border is open. You can leave now," the clerk says.

"Did you see my—" I can't say it. The pain is too much. "Did you see the guy I came in with?"

"Oh, he left several hours ago," she says, and that's when it hits me. I want to drop to my knees and cry, but I can't. I can't do that. I won't do that.

I move out to my bike and start it up. When I pass the shop his bike was at, I don't see it. He had to have it towed or they got it done early. I pass the sign that says Leaving Pandora, and I can't stop myself from pulling over. I look across the street to where his bike died. Where his bad luck started. But now I have the bad luck. He left me.

The ride back to Widow's Creek isn't as enjoyable as I normally find it. He took that from me too, along with my heart. Wind blows past my face, and I don't get the rush. I don't take the corners at dangerous speeds.

A couple of hours later, after taking my time, I pull into our driveway and head up to my room. Skyler is in school. Vixen is out somewhere, and I know Riddler is at the shop. I move to my bathroom off my bedroom and take a hot shower. My legs give out and I fall to the tile and cry. I scream in pain as my heart breaks apart.

"River." I hear Scout's voice, but I keep my head buried in my knees. I don't want to face the reality of the situation. I feel for a man who lies to everyone. I let her help me from the tub and dry me off.

She tucks me into bed and spoons against my back like she did after my parents died. Like I do for her when she thinks of Skyler's dad, Thad. He broke her heart too.

"He left me." I hiccup.

"Reaper?"

She knew. We've been best friends for a reason. We not only know each other so well, but we know when the other is hurting.

"He said he loved me and then left me. He said he wanted me. Said he'd protect us all." I cry harder as I think of everything he said, every promise he made.

"What happened there?"

I haven't told anyone what happened. I didn't call and let them know about the shoot-out. None of it.

"He killed Elias to save me. He protected me from Snake, who wanted me. He was so convincing."

"But?"

I take a deep breath and roll to face her. I can't

tell her it all. Something inside of me still wants to protect him.

"It was a trap. Snake wanted to get with me and then give me to Elias for his revenge. Reaper saved me. We ended up—" I can't finish the rest.

"I knew you liked him. Did he at least give you the big O?" She chuckles because she knows I've struggled with that because of how am.

I can't hide the blush. "Oh my god, did he. He knew." I flop my head into her chest. I go on to tell her in more detail about how Elias, or Crazy as he called himself, was there for revenge. I tell her I don't want to race for a while.

"I knew as soon as you let him near Sky that you liked him." She pats my back. "Want me to find out if he's at the Drago's clubhouse? We could go kick his ass." She pulls out her phone, and I slap my hand over it.

"No. Let it go."

"But, River."

"No." I roll from the bed and get dressed. I'm going to head to the studio to work.

"YOU NEED TO EAT." Vixen's voice breaks through the Taylor Swift music blaring through the speakers. It's another one of my guilty pleasures. She has a song for everything.

I wipe my hands on my cloth, grab the remote to turn down the music, and turn to look at her. She's holding a plate filled with roast beef, mashed potatoes, and green beans. One of my favorite comfort foods. I haven't come out of my studio for days. I've survived on water and granola bars.

I wave my hand at the wrappers. "I eat."

"That isn't food. Brazen said to tell you that she's got the girls searching for Snake." I wouldn't let Scout tell anyone about Reaper. As far as the club knows, I'm not racing because I'm traumatized from what happened with Elias and Snake, and that Reaper killed Elias when he drew a gun on me, but nothing else.

I'll take everything to my grave. The day after I got home, a judge from Pandora showed up. He gave me a statement saying that Klay married me of his own volition and would not grant me a divorce. That our wedding was validated with the court.

"This is beautiful." Vixen points at the painting on my easel as I shovel food into my mouth.

"I guess."

I look at the brooch that is the centerpiece held in the hands of a Druid priestess. I finished reading the journal. The priestess died lonely, and she didn't know that her love died on the ship crossing to the Americas. He never married anyone, and her name was the last thing on his lips. I'll never be able to break the curse and set them free because I can't love anyone else the way I loved Klay. It's why I keep his secret. It's how I know how the priestess felt when her love was ripped from her.

KLAY

Every night I watch her and wish I could go to her. My body is in withdrawals from her, and I'm barely hanging on. I've left everything and everyone. I have no one I can trust or talk to. I have to keep doing what I'm doing to protect her. That's all that matters.

I'm going to have to walk away for a while. I just pray that she forgives me someday for this. That she understands I had to do this to protect her. But she's a stubborn woman. It's going to take everything in me to make this right.

I took the farmer who gave me a ride to the plantation up on his offer to help me. The guy is a judge in Pandora. He made sure that the marriage certificate was filed with the courthouse and was all legal. I'm not letting her go.

I REALLY APPRECIATE you reading Off Balance. Please don't forget to leave a review. To continue reading more from the Devil's Handmaidens MC Alaska Chapter go to the series page. You can grab the next book in the series, Rattled. For a complete list of my books, along with series lists and reading orders on my website.

You might want to consider signing up for Surprises from E.M. for a free story as well as first chance at cover reveals, releases, contests and more.

Keep reading for a sneak peek of *Rattled*, the conclusion to Jinx and Reaper's story, coming in February 2024.

RATTLED

I stand by my Prez's side, taking in Thad and his friend, Dylan. I hate that Scout is going through this after her father was murdered. We came back home to Alaska. I left Kentucky with memories of a love I knew I'd never forget. I'm here to help Scout, as I always have. When Brazen made her the President of the Alaska chapter, I wasn't surprised. I was shocked, however, when Scout turned to me and made me her Vice President. This is my family and will always be. But watching both Badger and Scout having to relive what their loved ones did when they died is almost too much.

It looks like whoever killed Scout's dad killed Badger's sister, who has been missing for months.

"I asked you before if you had any enemies. We

have not been able to confirm if Mr. Smith is still being detained." Both of us stop breathing. I've battled Elias, and he met a bullet. But Phantom is still alive and in prison for almost killing Scout and attacking me.

"He isn't," a voice I never thought I'd hear again says.

"Reaper?"

I don't realize I'm in motion until he's standing in front of me. I rear back and swing. My hand cracks against his face in a loud smack that makes others gasp. I don't care. All I want to do is make him feel some of the pain he's made me feel for the last nine months. "What the fuck are you doing here?" I rail at him.

He rubs his cheek and chuckles. "Guess I deserved that."

"You fucking think. You left me. You fucking left me in that room." The tears are right there wanting to come out. Demanding to be let out, but I don't cry for him anymore. I can't.

"Baby." He moves to pull me into his body, but I'm aiming to hit him again. He stops me and holds me to him. "We have a lot to talk about. I came for you. I had to take care of business, and then I came for you."

"Well, go to hell. I don't want you." I yank away

from his grip and go stand with Scout. She's giving him the death glare. She helped pick me up after he broke me.

PreOrder Rattled Now.

ABOUT E.M.

E.M. Shue is an Alaskan award-winning romance author. She writes in many different sub-genres but always features badass heroines in gritty situations. As the mother to three grown daughters and two granddaughters she wants readers to be able to see that tough girls can have happy endings too. She is married to the love of her life of over twenty years who she married within months of starting to date, instalove is real.

She published her first book in 2017 after having a dream that later became the Beverley Award winning, Sniper's Kiss. Since her debut, she has gone on to win this award three more times with different books and has published over forty titles.

Join Surprises from E.M. to be kept up to date on all her new releases and appearances.

https://bit.ly/SurprisesfromEM

ALSO BY E.M. SHUE

Securities International Series

Sniper's Kiss: Book 1

Angel's Kiss: Book 2

Tougher Embrace: Book 2.5

Love's First Kiss: Book 3

Secret's Kiss: Book 4

Second Chance's Kiss: Book 5

Sniper's Kiss Goodnight: Book 5.5

Identity's Kiss: Book 6

Hope's Kiss: Book 7

Forever's Embrace: Book 7.5

Justice's Kiss: Book 8

Duchess's Kiss: Book 9

Kiss of Submission: Book 9.5

Truth's Kiss: Book 10

Kiss of Secret's Past: Book 10.5 (Coming July 2024)

Knights of Purgatory Syndicate

A Seductive Beauty

A Tortured Temptress

Santa Claus, Indiana Stories

Coal for Kiera: Christmas of Love Collaboration

Hanna's Valentine: A Santa Claus, Indiana Story

Hailey's Rodeo: A Santa Claus, Indiana Story

Love in a Small Town

Caine & Graco Saga

Accidentally Noah

Zeke's Choice

Lost in Linc

Completely Marco

Jackson Revealed

Trusting Jericho

Mafia Made

Her Empire: Mafia Made 2

His Rebel: Mafia Made 5

Her Exile: Mafia Made 8

Tattoos & Sin Series

Doctor Trouble

Vegas Jackpot

Doctor Sinful

Frozen Heart (Coming March 2024)

Stand-alones and Anthologies

Until Tucker: Happily Ever Alpha World

Until Lydia: Happily Ever Alpha World

Rocco's Atonement

Distracting David

Taliah's Warrant Officer

Forever Finn's Kisses

Discovering Tyler

Off Balance

Artfully Bred

Beyond The Temptation: Volume 2 (Blinded by Secrets) (Coming March 2024)

Devil's Handmaidens - Alaska

Wrecked

Rattled

Ruined (Coming November 2024)

Ramsey University Series

Virtuous

Tenacious (Coming April 2024)

Ambitious (Coming May 2024)

Russian Cardroom Series

Ante

Drawing Dead

All In (Coming June 2024)

Prominence Point Rescue Series

Confined Space

Grid Search (Coming September 2024)

Shiver of Chaos

Gambit's Property (Coming August 2024)

Printed in Great Britain
by Amazon